Penelope
and the Preposterous Birthday Party

written by
Sheri Radford

illustrated by
Christine Tripp

Lobster Press™

Penelope and the Preposterous Birthday Party
Text © 2009 Sheri Radford
Illustrations © 2009 Christine Tripp

Published by Lobster Press™
1620 Sherbrooke Street West, Suites C & D
Montréal, Québec   H3H 1C9
Tel. (514) 904-1100 • Fax (514) 904-1101
www.lobsterpress.com

Publisher: Alison Fripp
Editor: Meghan Nolan
Editorial Assistant: Emma Stephen
Graphic Design & Production: Tammy Desnoyers
Consultant on Font & Cover Design: Sara Gillingham

We acknowledge the financial support of the Government of Canada through the Book Publishing Industry Development Program (BPIDP) for our publishing activities.

The Canada Council | Le Conseil des Arts
for the Arts | du Canada

We acknowledge the support of the Canada Council for the Arts for our publishing program.

Library and Archives Canada Cataloguing in Publication

Radford, Sheri, 1971-
     Penelope and the preposterous birthday party / written by Sheri Radford ; illustrated by Christine Tripp.

(The Penelope series)
ISBN 978-1-897550-00-7 (bound).--ISBN 978-1-897550-24-3 (pbk.)

     I. Tripp, Christine II. Title. III. Series: Radford, Sheri, 1971- .
Penelope series.

PS8635.A337P456 2008   jC813'.6   C2008-902855-4

Printed and bound in Seoul, South Korea.

To Mom: Thanks for a childhood filled with love – and lots of fabulous birthday parties.

– *Sheri Radford*

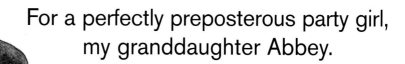

For a perfectly preposterous party girl, my granddaughter Abbey.

– *Christine Tripp*

Ding Dong.

Into the house streamed a horde of hyper children.

"Happy birthday, Penelope!"
they shouted.

"Penelope," said her mother, "I thought you were inviting just your closest friends to the party. This looks like your entire grade from school."

"I didn't want to leave anyone out," said Penelope.

Children were everywhere. They ran up and down the stairs.

They bounced on the sofa.

They stuck their fingers in the icing on the birthday cake
then smeared sticky fingers on the walls and furniture.

"Is this everyone?"
Penelope's father asked.

"Well, maybe just one or
two more," said Penelope.

"This party is outrageous,"
said Penelope's mother,
shaking her head.

A little boy ran by with a lampshade on his head,
chased by a little girl who was trying to show him her
flowered tights.

Ding Dong. Into the house streamed a score of soccer players and a bevy of ballet dancers.

"Happy birthday, Penelope!" they shouted.

"Penelope," said her mother, "I thought you were inviting just your closest friends to the party. This looks like your entire soccer team and all the kids from your ballet lessons."

"I didn't want to leave anyone out," said Penelope.

The ballet dancers pliéd

and jetéd through
the house.
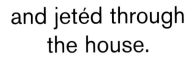

They kicked high kicks that knocked over knick-knacks.

The soccer players dribbled their balls through the
kitchen and took penalty shots in the living room.

"Is this everyone?"
Penelope's father asked.

"Well, maybe just two or
three more," said Penelope.

"This party is ridiculous,"

said Penelope's mother, rubbing her forehead.

A soccer player bounced a ball between his head and the ceiling. Two children swung from the chandelier.

Ding Dong.

Into the house streamed a multitude of monkeys and a crowd of clowns and a menagerie of magicians.

"Happy birthday, Penelope!"
they shouted.

"Penelope," said her mother, "I thought you were inviting just your closest friends to the party. This looks like all the people and all the animals from the circus we saw last weekend."

"I didn't want to leave anyone out," said Penelope.

A monkey and a trapeze artist swung from the ceiling fan.

A pony meandered through the kitchen and began
slurping from the punch bowl.

Nine clowns argued about whose turn it was to drive
the clown car.

"Is this everyone?"
Penelope's father asked.

"Well, maybe just three or four more," said Penelope.

Children stuffed
cotton candy into
their mouths and into
each other's ears.

A magician tried to
make a soccer player
disappear, but a ballet
dancer vanished instead.

An acrobat
somersaulted through
the house and out
the back door.

A giraffe ambled by the window, poked its head into
the second-floor bathroom, and began munching on
the aloe vera plant.

"This party is preposterous!"

Penelope's mother shouted over the noise, rubbing her forehead again. A sticky, crying child clung to one of her legs, and a sticky, chattering monkey clung to the other.

"This party is **fabulous**! Next year's will be even better!" Penelope shouted back.

"Next year you'll invite just four or five of your closest friends to the party," Penelope's mother corrected firmly.

Penelope and her parents watched a trio of horses prance around the yard. They watched a troupe of trapeze artists swing from the clothesline. They watched an elephant sit on the patio furniture, squashing it flat.

"This party *is* preposterous,"
Penelope whispered to herself.

She turned to her parents.

"Okay, next year I won't invite the elephant!"